EAGLE BOY

For my son, Sam,
Whose spirit shines like a great soaring eagle!
—R.L.V.

For my sons, Matt and Wade.
—L.C.

A NOTE ABOUT THIS TALE
The legend of Eagle Boy has long been told along the Pacific Northwest coast.
From the Quinault and Makah in the south to the Haida and Tlingit in the north, many Native
American tribes have their own versions of the story. Even that notorious trickster Raven is featured
in one retelling in which he, of course, is the hero. Yet, no matter the source or whether the tale is
written or spoken, a common thread prevails of a boy befriending the majestic eagle.
Their relationship demonstrates to all people the values of friendship and trust—underscored
in this version by the power of forgiveness between the boy and his people. These are
the qualities that appealed to me when I first heard the tale.
—R.L.V.

Text copyright ©2000 by Richard Lee Vaughan
Illustrations copyright ©2000 by Lee Christiansen

Cover and interior design: Karen Schober
Printed in Hong Kong

Distributed in Canada by Raincoast Books, Ltd.
04 03 02 01 00   5 4 3 2 1

Library of Congress Cataloging in Publication Data
Vaughan, Richard Lee, 1947-
        Eagle Boy: a Pacific Northwest tale/Richard Lee Vaughan; illustrated by Lee Christiansen.
        p.   cm.
        Summary: An Indian boy's friendship with eagles ultimately saves his village in the Pacific Northwest
        from starvation.
        ISBN 1-57061-171-8 (alk. paper)
        1. Indians of North America—Northwest, Pacific—Juvenile fiction. [1. Indians of North America—
        Northwest, Pacific—Fiction. 3. Northwest, Pacific—Fiction.]
        I. Christiansen, Lee, ill. II. Title.
        PZ7.V4525 Eag   2000
        [E]—dc21   00-029663

Sasquatch Books
615 Second Avenue
Seattle, Washington 98104
(206) 467-4300
www.SasquatchBooks.com
books@SasquatchBooks.com

EAGLE BOY

A
PACIFIC NORTHWEST
NATIVE TALE

RETOLD BY
RICHARD LEE VAUGHAN

ILLUSTRATED BY
LEE CHRISTIANSEN

SASQUATCH BOOKS
SEATTLE

Along the rugged shoreline of the Pacific Northwest, a village stood on the cliffs overlooking the ocean. Eagles with snow-white heads and sleek, dark bodies swooped over the village. With razor-sharp talons, they snatched silver fish from the water.

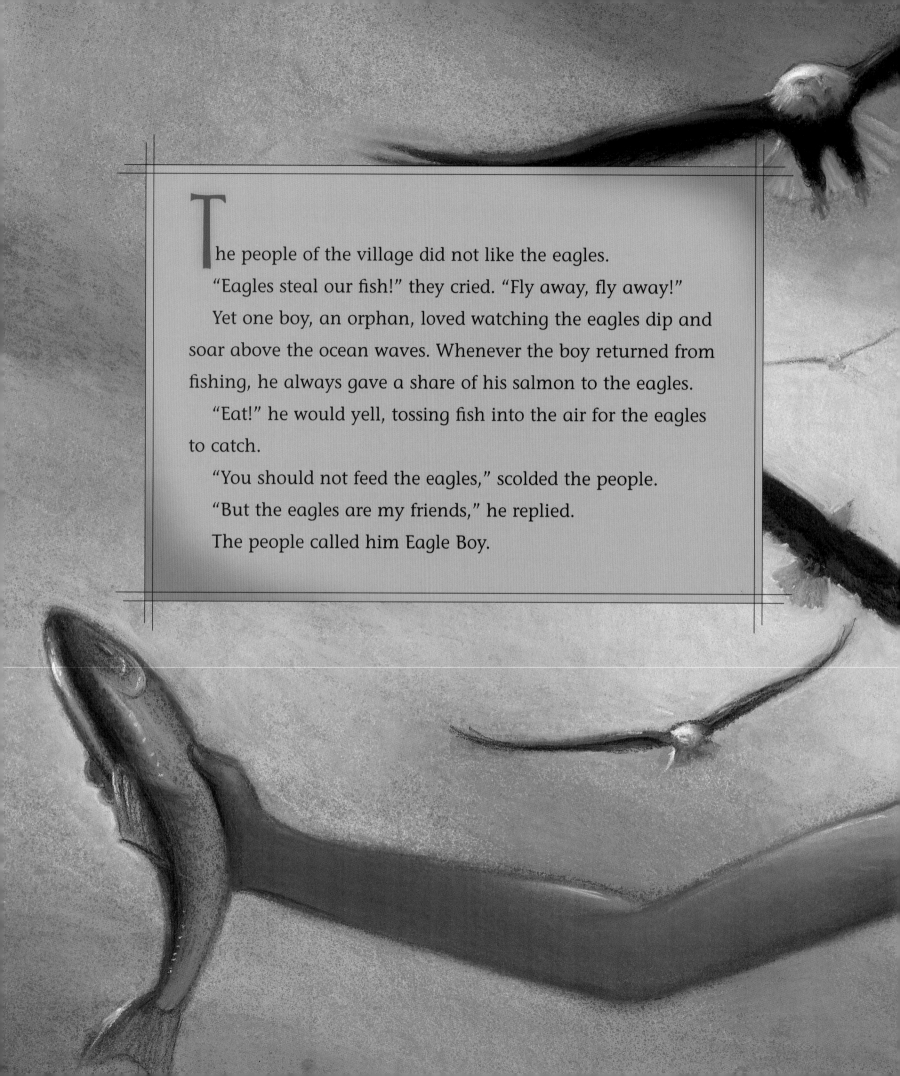

The people of the village did not like the eagles.

"Eagles steal our fish!" they cried. "Fly away, fly away!"

Yet one boy, an orphan, loved watching the eagles dip and soar above the ocean waves. Whenever the boy returned from fishing, he always gave a share of his salmon to the eagles.

"Eat!" he would yell, tossing fish into the air for the eagles to catch.

"You should not feed the eagles," scolded the people.

"But the eagles are my friends," he replied.

The people called him Eagle Boy.

Eagle Boy was a good fisherman. In summer months, when fish were plentiful, he offered his largest and finest fish to the chief's eldest daughter, Kwish-kwish-ee.

"I do not need your fish," she said, mocking him.

One year, as autumn faded into winter, fish became scarce, and the whole village began to run short of food.

"We must move our village," announced the chief. "We must find more food."

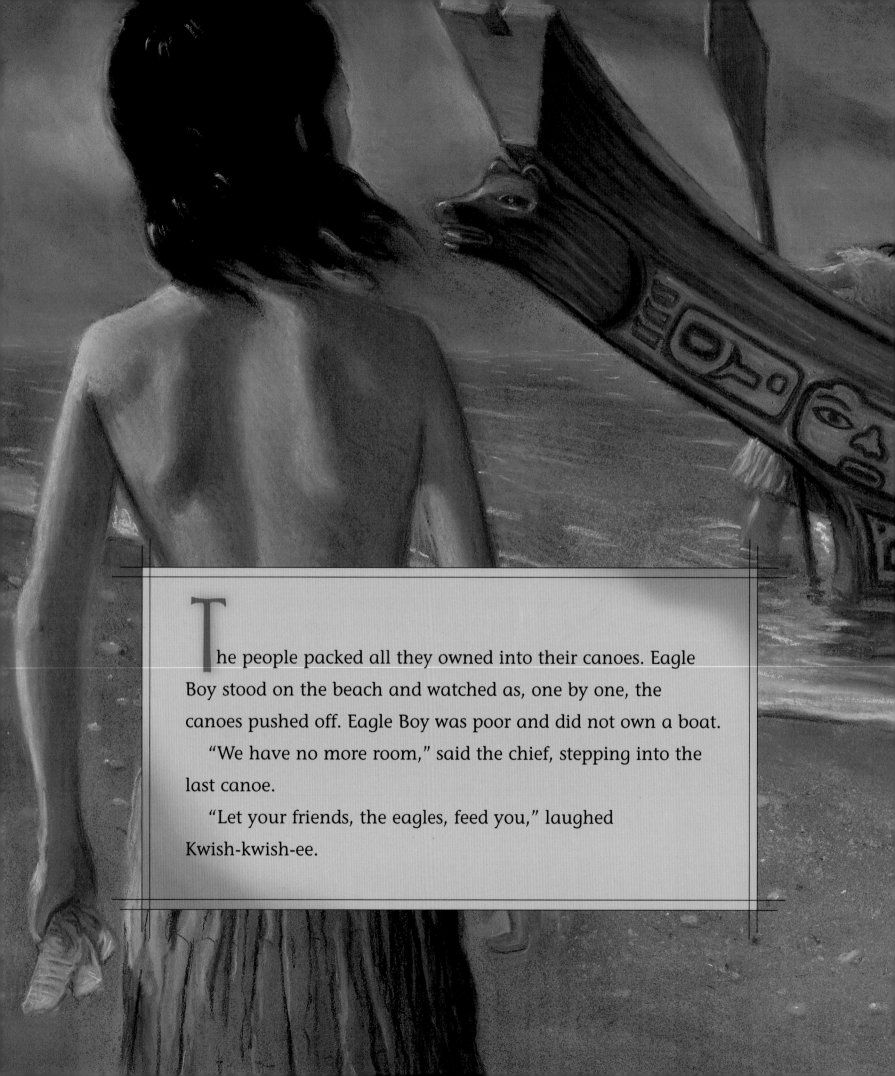

The people packed all they owned into their canoes. Eagle Boy stood on the beach and watched as, one by one, the canoes pushed off. Eagle Boy was poor and did not own a boat.

"We have no more room," said the chief, stepping into the last canoe.

"Let your friends, the eagles, feed you," laughed Kwish-kwish-ee.

ut just before they paddled away, the chief's youngest
daughter, Chuh-coo-duh-bee, slipped Eagle Boy a piece of dried
fish so he would not get hungry.

As the canoes disappeared over the waves, Eagle Boy stood
alone on the windswept beach.

He ate his small piece of dried fish and fell asleep to the sound of waves crashing against the shore.

That night he dreamed of eagles. Eagles soaring in the sunshine. Eagles swooping over large piles of fish. He even dreamed that he too could fly.

EAGLE BOY

For my son, Sam,
Whose spirit shines like a great soaring eagle!
—R.L.V.

For my sons, Matt and Wade.
—L.C.

A NOTE ABOUT THIS TALE
The legend of Eagle Boy has long been told along the Pacific Northwest coast.
From the Quinault and Makah in the south to the Haida and Tlingit in the north, many Native
American tribes have their own versions of the story. Even that notorious trickster Raven is featured
in one retelling in which he, of course, is the hero. Yet, no matter the source or whether the tale is
written or spoken, a common thread prevails of a boy befriending the majestic eagle.
Their relationship demonstrates to all people the values of friendship and trust—underscored
in this version by the power of forgiveness between the boy and his people. These are
the qualities that appealed to me when I first heard the tale.
—R.L.V.

Cover and interior design: Karen Schober
Printed in Hong Kong

Distributed in Canada by Raincoast Books, Ltd.
04 03 02 01 00   5 4 3 2 1

Library of Congress Cataloging in Publication Data
Vaughan, Richard Lee, 1947-
        Eagle Boy: a Pacific Northwest tale/Richard Lee Vaughan; illustrated by Lee Christiansen.
        p. cm.
        Summary: An Indian boy's friendship with eagles ultimately saves his village in the Pacific Northwest
        from starvation.
        ISBN 1-57061-171-8 (alk. paper)
        1. Indians of North America—Northwest, Pacific—Juvenile fiction. [1. Indians of North America—
        Northwest, Pacific—Fiction. 3. Northwest, Pacific—Fiction.]
        I. Christiansen, Lee, ill. II. Title.
        PZ7.V4525 Eag   2000
        [E]—dc21   00-029663

Sasquatch Books
615 Second Avenue
Seattle, Washington 98104
(206) 467-4300
www.SasquatchBooks.com
books@SasquatchBooks.com

EAGLE BOY

A
Pacific Northwest
Native Tale

Retold by
RICHARD LEE VAUGHAN

ILLUSTRATED BY
LEE CHRISTIANSEN

SASQUATCH BOOKS
SEATTLE

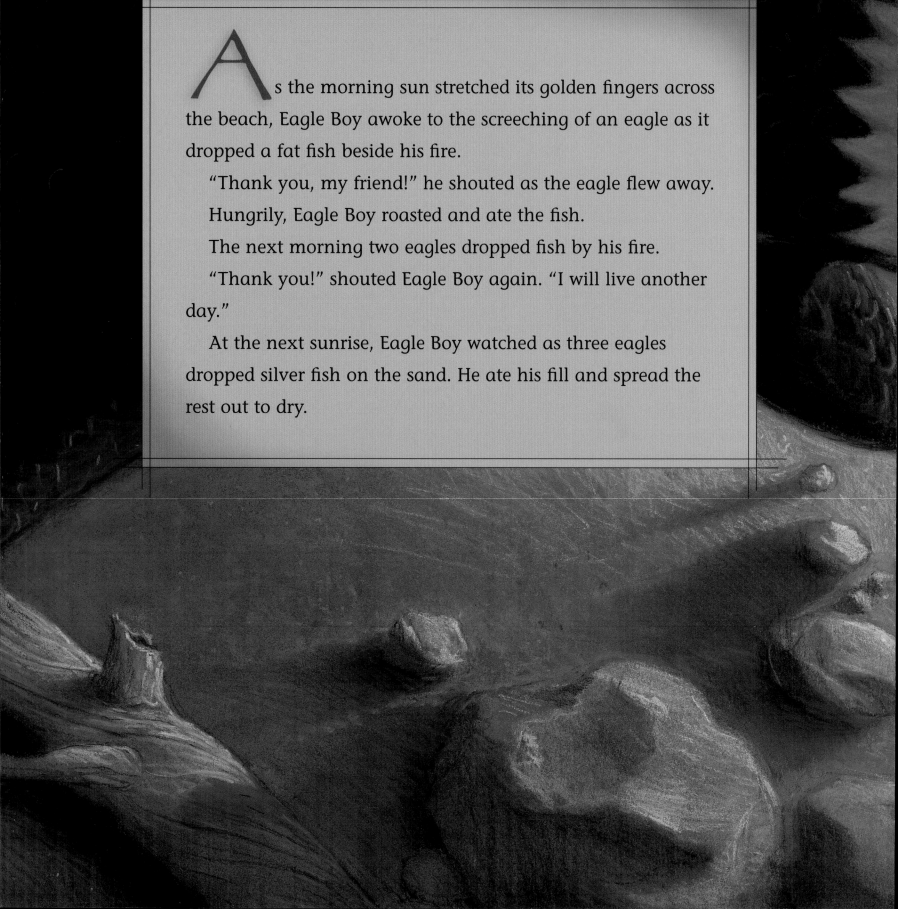

As the morning sun stretched its golden fingers across the beach, Eagle Boy awoke to the screeching of an eagle as it dropped a fat fish beside his fire.

"Thank you, my friend!" he shouted as the eagle flew away.

Hungrily, Eagle Boy roasted and ate the fish.

The next morning two eagles dropped fish by his fire.

"Thank you!" shouted Eagle Boy again. "I will live another day."

At the next sunrise, Eagle Boy watched as three eagles dropped silver fish on the sand. He ate his fill and spread the rest out to dry.

When evening approached, Eagle Boy gathered all the wood he could find and built an enormous bonfire on the beach. Dancing around and around the flames, he sang songs to honor the eagles.

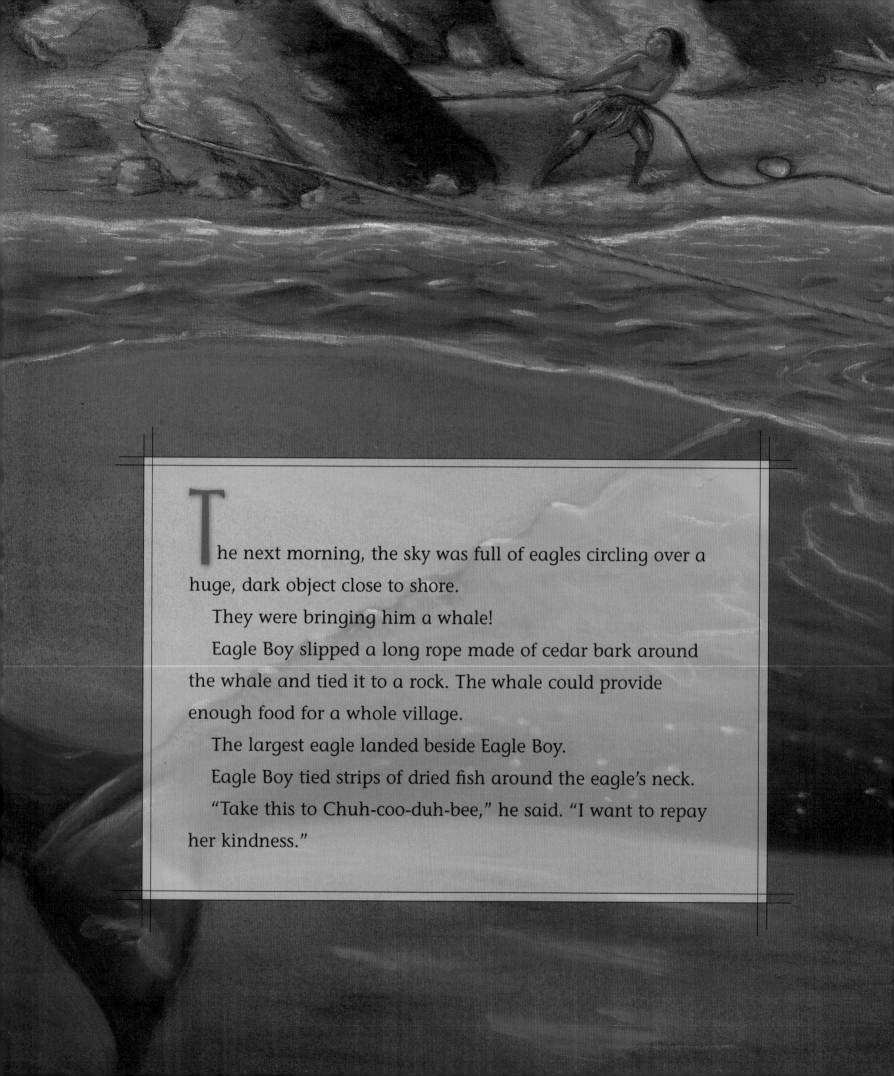

The next morning, the sky was full of eagles circling over a huge, dark object close to shore.

They were bringing him a whale!

Eagle Boy slipped a long rope made of cedar bark around the whale and tied it to a rock. The whale could provide enough food for a whole village.

The largest eagle landed beside Eagle Boy.

Eagle Boy tied strips of dried fish around the eagle's neck.

"Take this to Chuh-coo-duh-bee," he said. "I want to repay her kindness."

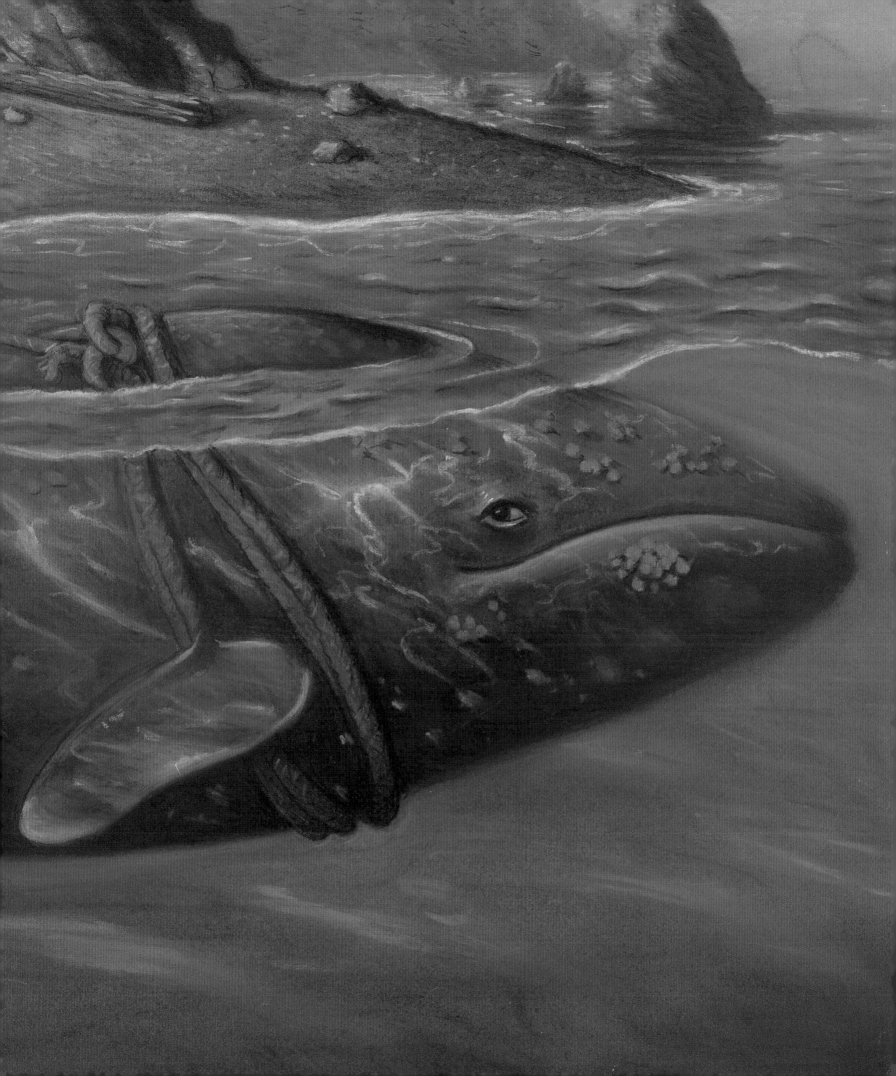

Gliding on the wind, the Great Eagle found the tribe huddled around a campfire on a distant beach. Hunting and fishing had not been good. The shadow of hunger showed on the people's faces.

The eagle landed beside Chuh-coo-duh-bee as she dug hopefully for clams on the beach. She realized at once who had sent the food.

Taking the dried fish from the eagle, she gobbled a few bites and then raced to her father.

"Look!" she cried. "A gift from Eagle Boy!"

Kwish-kwish-ee eyed the fish with greed. "The boy you left behind is rich with food," she said to the chief, "while we have nothing. Take us back, Father! I will marry the boy, and we will eat his food."

The chief shook his head in shame. "We were wrong to leave the boy."

The people around the campfire agreed.

"We thought only of ourselves," said one man.

"The boy will not accept us back," said another.

"Even if he did," said an old woman, "we could never make the journey home without food."

Perched on a branch high above the them, the Great Eagle listened to the people. Spreading its giant wings, it returned across the water.

That night, Eagle Boy stood before the Great Eagle. The eagle's intense eyes were dark pools of wisdom. Deep in those eyes, the boy could see a distant beach where his people sat weak with hunger.

Eagle Boy turned toward the flames. "Let them go hungry!" he shouted in anger. "Just as they left me to do."

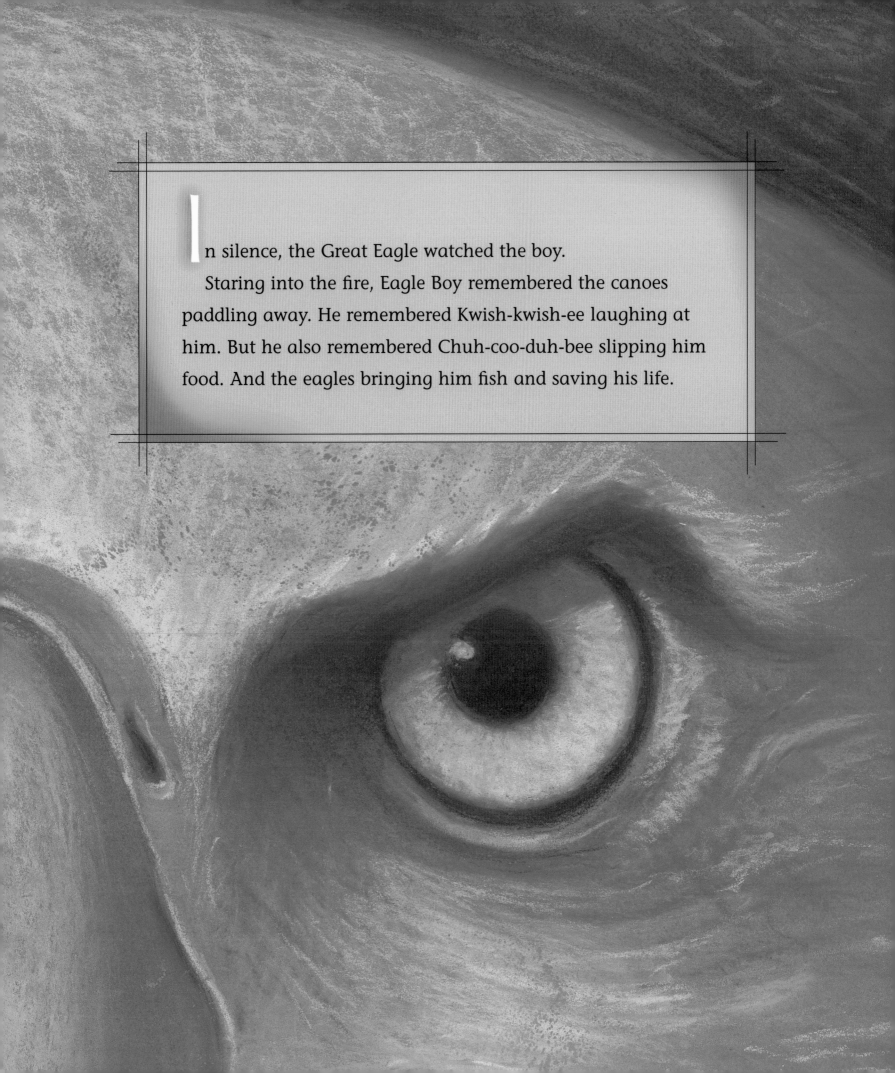

In silence, the Great Eagle watched the boy.

Staring into the fire, Eagle Boy remembered the canoes paddling away. He remembered Kwish-kwish-ee laughing at him. But he also remembered Chuh-coo-duh-bee slipping him food. And the eagles bringing him fish and saving his life.

At dawn the boy again stood before the Great Eagle. "How can I help my people?" he asked.

The eagle spread its wings and lifted into the air. As it rose, one shiny black feather fell, floating down toward Eagle Boy.

The boy reached out and caught the feather. As he did, a wave of power flowed through him, and in that moment the boy took the form of an eagle.

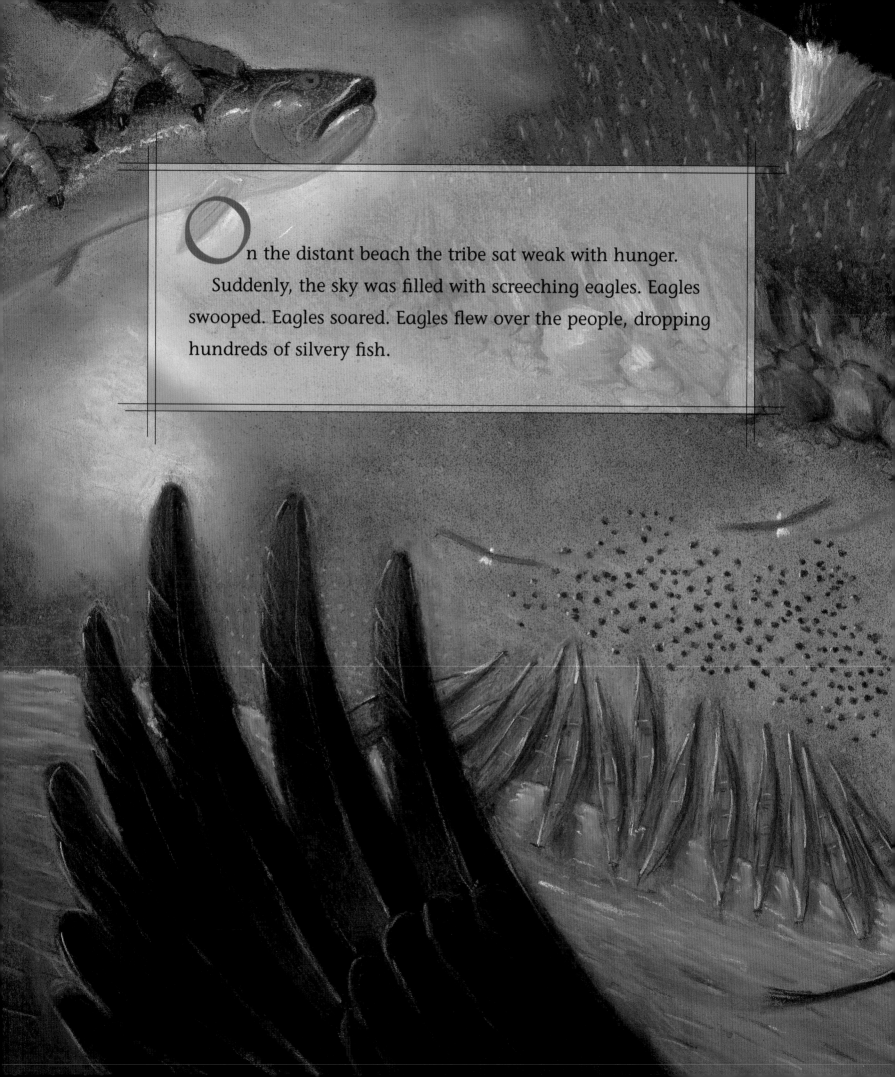

On the distant beach the tribe sat weak with hunger. Suddenly, the sky was filled with screeching eagles. Eagles swooped. Eagles soared. Eagles flew over the people, dropping hundreds of silvery fish.

It is a sign from Eagle Boy!" cried Chuh-coo-duh-bee, smiling.

"Yes," agreed the chief. "He has forgiven us. Now we can go home."

With renewed strength, the people packed their canoes and set out across the water.

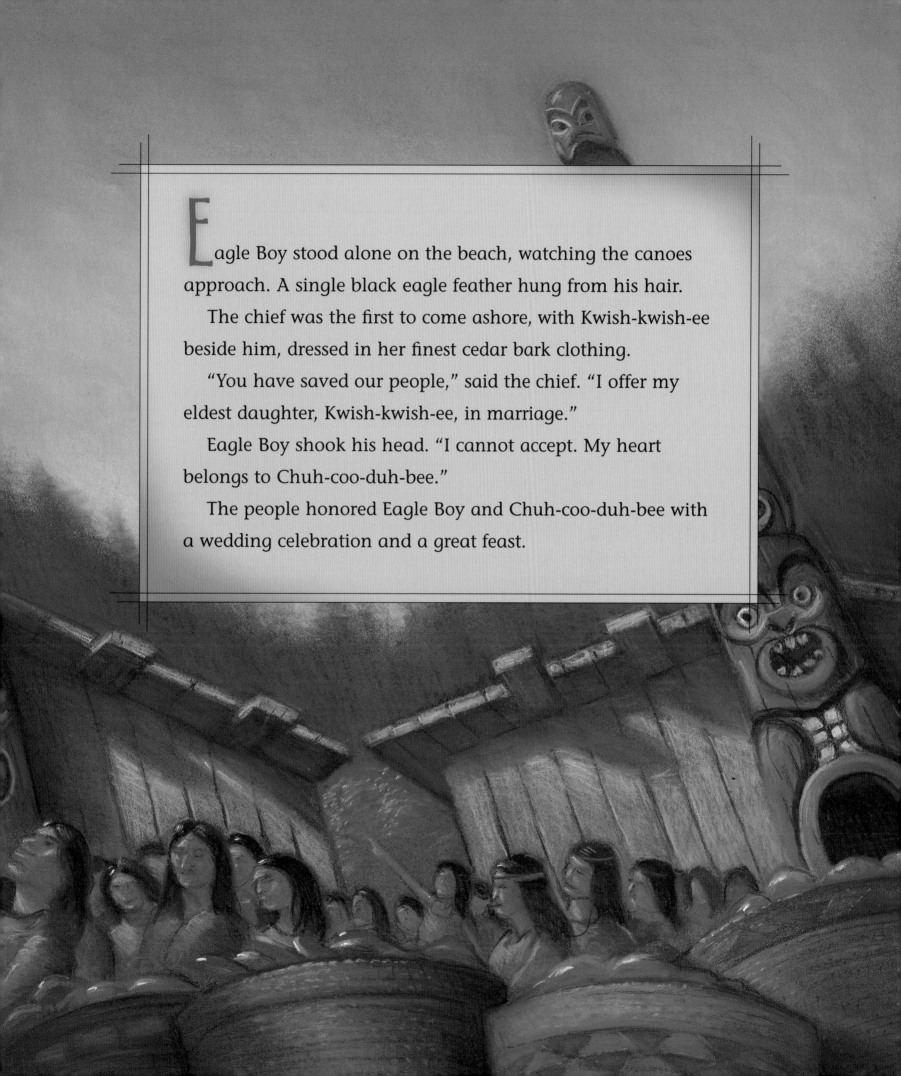

Eagle Boy stood alone on the beach, watching the canoes approach. A single black eagle feather hung from his hair.

The chief was the first to come ashore, with Kwish-kwish-ee beside him, dressed in her finest cedar bark clothing.

"You have saved our people," said the chief. "I offer my eldest daughter, Kwish-kwish-ee, in marriage."

Eagle Boy shook his head. "I cannot accept. My heart belongs to Chuh-coo-duh-bee."

The people honored Eagle Boy and Chuh-coo-duh-bee with a wedding celebration and a great feast.